Pucker Power
The Super-powered Superpug

Kevin
Stevens

Illustrated by
Sheena Dempsey

Little Island

Ted*

Clare**

* Dad   ** Mum

Suzie

JP

The
Powers

Pucker*

*The dog

PUCKER POWER: The Super-powered Superpug

First published in 2015 by
Little Island Books
7 Kenilworth Park
Dublin 6W
Ireland
www.littleisland.ie

ISBN: 978-1-910411-30-8

A British Library Cataloguing in Publication record for this book is available from the British Library.

Cover design by Sheena Dempsey
Typset by Gráinne Clear in Georgia (by Matthew Carter), with titles in Justy (by Justin Brown) and Minya (by Ray Larabie)

Printed in Poland by Drukarnia Skleniars

Little Island receives financial assistance from the Arts Council (An Chomhairle Ealaíon) and the Arts Council of Northern Ireland.

10 9 8 7 6 5 4 3 2 1

Thanks

Super-slobbery thank-yous to the hooper zeroes who helped Pucker save the day: Alicia Estibenz, Gráinne Clear and Siobhán Parkinson. And to the wonderful Sheena Dempsey, whose doggie drawings are the best.

For the children of Chajul... who love Espike.
(KS)

For Aoife and Darragh
(SD)

1

Puckermania

'Bad dog, Pucker! *Dad bog.*'

JP pulled hard on the lead, but Pucker's tough little legs pulled harder. Tongue hanging out, ears flapping like furry butterflies, Pucker would not stay on the footpath.

All over St Stephen's Green were big black signs with big white letters:

STAY OFF THE GRASS

Did they think dogs could read?

'Pucker!' JP was still shouting. 'Stop it. Eating daffodils makes you sick. You *know* that.'

But Pucker Power had a mind of his own. And the lead was the stretchy kind that unspooled from the handle like a fishing line. JP had no control. So Pucker did whatever he wanted – eat the flowers, drink from the fountain, scare the ducks, dig a hole in the grass, lift his leg against one of … one of the black signs?

'Pucker!'

Too late. The sign shone wetly in the February sun.

It wasn't fair. JP's sister, Suzie, had a piano recital at the Academy of Music, and that was all the Power parents could talk about. *Isn't Suzie brilliant*, and *Isn't Suzie talented* and *What would we do without Suzie*. Suzie, who didn't even have any powers. While JP had to wrestle with Pucker for an hour and stop him from destroying the most flowerful, dog-un-friendly park in Dublin.

And what was worse, tomorrow was JP's birthday and no-one in the family had even mentioned it. Could they actually forget his birthday?

Ahead, two men wearing white overalls and painters' caps pulled low over their foreheads were painting a lamppost. They both had thick glasses and bushy moustaches and spoke in a foreign language. One of them was on the foot-path, holding the ladder firm. The other was high up the rungs, stretching to paint the light fixture.

There was a can of green paint hanging from the top of the ladder. More cans of paint were on the ground, along with a spotted cloth, a pile of brushes and a big wooden box with holes in it.

Pucker froze – still as a statue except for his ears twitching and the fur on his neck rising. JP grew nervous. This was not good. This was how Puckermania started.

Remember, JP – no flying. These had been his mum's last words before the rest of the family headed off to hear Suzie's piano recital.

Easy for *Mum* to say. What about now, when the safest thing for JP to do would be to pick up Pucker and zoom off, away from all trouble? Because it was perfectly plain that he did not like the painters. Was it the caps and the overalls? They looked sort of like a uniform. And, oh, how Pucker hated uniforms!

A trembling stare. A very low growl. His back legs tensed and then exploded into a blur of motion.

In an instant he had the hem of one painter's trousers in his powerful jaws and was thrashing and pulling like a tiny tugboat. JP yanked hard on the lead and dug his heels into the lawn. No use. He grabbed Pucker by the legs and pulled and pulled. Still no use. This was a mutt on a mission.

The painter yelled and screamed and shook his leg. His glasses went flying and his cap fell over his eyes. But he didn't let go of the ladder, which trembled and tilted as he battled to free his leg from Pucker's grasp. At the top, the other painter was like an acrobat on a high wire, twisting and turning his body and waving his arms as he tried not to fall. Both men were yelling in their language, which had lots of *zh* and *shch* sounds. JP didn't understand a word, but he was pretty sure there was some cursing in there.

The painter's trousers ripped, and dog and boy tumbled into a heap on the grass. A piece of white cloth hung from Pucker's teeth as he yelped and struggled in JP's arms. JP wouldn't let Pucker go, though.

Through the whirl of fur and legs JP saw the other painter, the one on the top of the ladder, teeter and totter and lose his footing, so that he came down head-first on top of his partner.

Their heads met with an almighty crack ... followed by the ladder clattering on top of them ... followed at once by the full can of paint, which spilled its thick liquid over their hats and overalls and moustaches. JP couldn't help but notice that the paint matched the lovely grass of St Stephen's Green.

Remember, JP – it was his dad's voice this time, in JP's mind – *if you get into trouble and it's your fault, the best thing to do is to own up, admit your mistake, and face it like a man.*

So JP legged it.

But he didn't have a choice. Really he didn't. Because Pucker had already taken off, tearing across the grass, ploughing through the flowers and knocking over two of the black signs.

It was JP's job to protect his pet. But Pucker wasn't plummeting across the park and causing even more damage because he was afraid of getting into trouble. No. There was something on the other side of the fountain that had attracted his attention.

For the first time in his doggie life, Pucker Power had found something more exciting than a uniform.

2

Puppy Love

As he raced round the fountain, JP saw that Pucker had come to a stop beside the stone bridge that arched over the pond. His tail was wagging furiously, and his tongue hung from his panting mouth like a piece of washing on a clothesline. In front of him, her button nose in the air, her small mouth pursed, was a stylish black poodle wearing a diamond-studded collar, a fringed tartan doggie coat, and a pink bow in her perfectly groomed fur.

She was not impressed. And neither was her owner, a girl of about JP's age in a red coat, white scarf and blue beret.

Both girl and poodle looked away from Pucker, their faces scrunched up in disgust, their eyes aimed somewhere high above the fountain, obviously hoping that this whining, slobbering pug with a squashed face and goo-goo eyes and the silly boy that owned him would just ... go ... away.

But the air around Pucker's head was throbbing with little hearts. Even JP could see it. The pug was in love. Plainly.

At least he was easy to grab now. JP caught him by the collar and re-attached the lead.

'I'm sorry,' he said, looking up at the girl with the poodle. Her nails were painted a red that matched her coat and a tiny silver earring quivered beside her clenched jaw. 'He got away from me.'

'Is that so? He got away from you?'

JP had started studying French in school, so he recognised the accent. And because he had a big sister, he also knew the language of sarcasm.

Iz zat so? JP mocked in his mind. But on the outside he was laughing nervously. 'A bundle of energy is this little fella. A devil to keep on the lead.'

And Pucker was doing his best to prove it, straining against JP's grip, trying to give the poodle an affectionate smooch with his dripping tongue.

When he got a little too close, the girl pointed at him and screamed, 'Keep that awful creature away from my precious Penelope.'

Penelope, startled by her owner's outburst, hid behind the girl's legs and yapped. An evil, tiny-dog yap. But music to Pucker's ears. He kept pulling away from JP, trying to plant a kiss on the poodle's snarling lips.

'Ah, he's no harm,' JP said, struggling to hold his temper as well as the lead. 'Really he isn't. He gets on with all dogs, so he does, and he's very clean. I gave him a bath this morning.'

The girl looked at JP with true horror. Of course. She would have servants to bathe her precious little Penelope, wouldn't she, and special groomers with degrees from French beauty schools for poodles, and a doggie dress designer and a doggie jeweller.

'I have no time for such nonsense,' the girl said dramatically, looking at her watch. 'I am late, and it is the fault of you, you and this – beast. I must meet my parents at the Shelbourne Hotel in *cinq minutes*. We are going to the rugby match and we must be on time. We are guests of honour.'

Really, JP wanted to say, *guests of honour? Well, I can fly.* But before he could say a word he saw the two painters, green-skinned and bug-eyed, their hats and glasses gone, heading towards him like lions after a gazelle. One had a big sheet in his hands and the other carried the wooden box with holes in it.

There was only one thing for it. Time for super- powers!

JP bundled Pucker into his arms and went

into fly mode. But he didn't have his cape – and when JP was capeless, anything could happen!

He took off all right, but couldn't control his flight path. *Whang* – he flew right into a tree. Head first. Fireworks in his eyes, stars around his skull, birds twittering in his ears. Not real birds. Cuckoo-clock birds. *Coo-koo. Coo-koo.*

He lifted his groggy head, expecting to be grabbed by the painters and given a good hiding.

But they weren't grabbing him. They were grabbing the girl. The first man threw the sheet over her head and knocked her to the ground, while the other snatched the poodle and thrust it into the wooden box. Pucker leapt from JP's arms and went to the rescue of his beloved Penelope. But this time the painter was ready for him – using a second sheet, he wrapped Pucker up and threw him into the fountain.

The man kept shouting in his language. '*Vee gloopo mallinkaya sobochka ... Vee gloopo mallinkaya sobochka ...*'

JP shook the stars from his eyes. Pucker! They were drowning his little Puckerstuck!

But in a flash the dog escaped from the sheet,

climbed out of the fountain and, dripping wet, jumped back into the fray, lunging for the painter in full Puckermania again.

But this man knew what he was doing. Swivelling like a bullfighter, he grabbed the doggie by his collar, lifted him in a high circle, and thrust him into the wooden box, beside Penelope. *Thump, thwack, click*. Like that the box was locked, lifted onto the men's shoulders and whisked away.

Silence.

Except for the muffled cries of the French girl as she unwound the sheet that bound her. A light rain was falling. Scattered around the fountain were devastated daffodils, pulverised pansies and shredded sheet.

It had all happened so quickly. Both dogs gone. Nothing left of the men but a trail of green footprints up and over the stone bridge.

Wide-eyed and breathless, the girl gasped. 'What ...? Where ...? *Penelope!*'

She ran to JP, who had struggled to his feet. She seemed to have forgotten how much she disliked him.

'What has happened?' she cried. 'Where is my precious one?'

His head still pounded and his vision was fuzzy, but JP knew what he had seen. Fighting back tears, he said, 'Pucker and Penelope. They've both been *nog-dapped*!'

3

Parlez-vous Parfait?

Pearse Street Garda Station was a zoo. A herd of hairy buffalos dressed in rugby uniforms. An older French couple, sleek as jaguars. Street kids whooping it up like monkeys, while a red-faced sergeant, squealing like the little piggy who went wee-wee-wee all the way home, chased them out of the door.

Into this chaos came the Power family, looking for JP. Ted Power like a codfish, his chin thrust out, his teeth bared. JP's mum, Clare, eyes wide as a deer's. And Suzie, an angry sparrow, chirping crossly because her special music day had been ruined.

It had been so humiliating. JP had rung their mum's mobile in the middle of Suzie's piano performance. He rang from the station, crying his head off and making no sense. The family had rushed out of the academy hall, Suzie's beautiful phrases from Mozart completely forgotten. Typical of JP. Absolutely typical. He couldn't even take the dog for a walk without creating a disaster.

JP was sitting at a desk in the station's back office, his hair sticking up. A garda held an ice pack to his head, mooning at him as if he were her long-lost baby boy.

'The poor little chap,' she said. 'He got an awful knock on the head. Do you want another ice-pop, JP?'

'I'm fine for the moment, thanks very much.'

JP spoke in that weak, whiney voice he put on when he was milking sympathy.

The garda lifted the ice, revealing a lump the size of a tangerine. Banged his head trying to fly, no doubt.

No sooner did they see him than Suzie's parents were stuck to JP like a wet shirt.

'Are you all right, pet?'

'That's some lump you have.'

'We were mortified when the guards rang.'

'Is there anything we can get you?'

'Where's Pucker?' Suzie said, in a flat, bored voice.

Her dad looked around the room. 'Yes. Where is that little rascal?'

JP's face crumpled like an old newspaper. He started crying. 'He ... he ... he's been ...'

Across the room, a red-white-and-blue girl wailed, *'Ma Penelope!'*

French, Suzie thought. *The couple must be her parents.*

'Excusez-moi?' said the dad, leaning in to the Powers. About Ted's age, he was dressed in an expensive suit, silk tie and pointed black leather

shoes. A very elegant man, with perfectly parted hair, but a face like a tin opener. 'You are the family of the pug, no?'

Ted looked the man up and down, brushing sandwich crumbs from the stomach of his snot-green Dunnes Stores jumper. 'If you mean Pucker, then, yes, the pooch is a Power. And more pucker to him for being a power is what I always say.'

Ted laughed maniacally, the Frenchman stared, Suzie cringed.

'My daughter, Paulette,' the Frenchman said, pointing at the weeping girl, who was clutching her mother, 'she has told us how brave your son is today. You must be *varry* proud.'

They all looked at JP. He was picking his nose.

'We have raised our boy,' Ted said, 'always to do the right thing. Er, what *did* he do?'

'His varry best I would say,' the Frenchman said, raising his hands. 'Though, alas, it did not stop the villains from their evil ways.'

At the mention of evil and villains, Ted heated up, wisps of smoke curling from his ears. He was having more and more trouble controlling his super-fire these days. 'Villains, you say? Mischief? Arch-criminals needing to be taught a lesson?'

JP wailed. 'The bad men took Pucker away in a booden wox!'

The red-faced sergeant, returning from another shouting match with kids from the road, stopped in his tracks, eyeing up Ted and sniffing the smoke. 'Sweet Jaypers. What are *you* doing here?'

'Here to serve, sergeant, here to serve.'

'Now listen here, you Powers, you just stay out of this. The daughter of this distinguished French gentleman here is upset, very upset. Her pedigree poodle's gone missing, and the last thing we need is you and your so-called super-powers creating another international incident.'

'But, sergeant,' the Frenchman said, pointing at JP, 'this family also ...'

'Also what?'

'Their *chien* ... how you say? Kidnapped? Dognapped?'

JP and Paulette cried in chorus.

'What!' yelped Clare.

'Poor Pucker,' shouted Suzie.

'Oh, no,' said the sergeant.

'Oh, yes,' said Ted, folding his arms. 'But never fear, the Powers are here.'

Penelope's owner, it appeared, was named Paulette Parfait. Paulette's dad, Pierre, was president of the French Rugby Federation. Her mum, Patricia, was a famous ex-model with a perfect nose and a mouth that didn't know how to smile. Clare was trying to be nice to Mrs Parfait and getting nowhere. Suzie could see that her mum would much prefer to be planting flowers in her garden than stuck here with a bunch of French snobs. And all Suzie wanted to do was play the piano.

Mrs Parfait certainly wasn't giving her hysterical daughter much attention. Paulette was beside herself, but her mother was beside the radio, listening to coverage of the Ireland–France rugby international being played at the Aviva Stadium. The doggie crisis meant that the family was at the garda station instead of the match, and every few minutes Mrs Parfait would glide across the floor and whisper the score in her husband's ear. With every whisper, he grew more irritated. Ireland was winning.

The French team had sent along several beefy, unshaven substitutes to support the Parfaits, and with every update on the score, Mr Parfait would glare at them, as if it were their fault. They cowered like scared chickens, even though any one of them could have knocked over their boss with a baby finger.

'We must do something, *now*!' Mr Parfait shouted, though Suzie wasn't sure if he was talking about the dognapping or the rugby match.

'I'll tell you what we *don't* do,' Ted said, a finger in the air. 'We don't lie around here like a bunch of stand-byers wondering what to do next. We are the Powers. Fighting crime is what we do. I ask you – can a leopard change his stripes?'

But Mr Parfait wasn't listening. His mobile rang. He answered, went silent and turned deathly pale.

'*Oui … oui … oui.*' He hung up and said in a

21

whisper. 'They have the dogs.'

'Who has?'

'The evil men. And they want – *ten million euro.*'

The station went silent. The words echoed around the room: ten million euro. It was like something from a film. In the quiet, the radio blared: *And that's the match – what a victory for Ireland!*

Everyone stared at Mr Parfait. For once, the rugby match did not worry him. 'I must go to the Luxembourg Gardens tomorrow. At nine o'clock. Someone will meet me at the Medici Fountain, by the statue of Polyphemus, with instructions. Any police and they will … they will …' He looked at his daughter and said no more.

Finally he turned to the sergeant. 'Thank you for your help, sergeant. I know that as a man of honour you will say nothing until after my meeting. Of course I will inform the French police in time, but first I must meet these ….' He paused, then turned to Ted and Clare.

'We'll come with you,' Clare said.

'*Non, non, non,*' Mr Parfait said excitedly.

'This is our responsibility. Do not fear – I will make sure to find and return Poo-care.'

'Pucker?'

'That's what I said – Poo-care.'

'But we're the *Powers*,' Ted said. 'Take us with you and we'll get those little pooches back before you can say *merci beaucoup*. We'll capture those dastardly dognappers if it's the first thing we do.'

But Mr Parfait was already on his way out the door with his family, followed by the thundering rugby herd.

'Wait!' Ted shouted.

Suzie said to her mum, 'Does that mean we have to come up with five million for Pucker?'

'I'll tell you what it means,' Ted said, puffing out his chest.

Smoke was now pouring from his ears, his neck, his hair – and before he could say anything else the fire alarm went off. Guards from all over the building streamed out of the back room and headed for the front door. The urchins from the road had sneaked back in, and were laughing and running through the legs of the adults. A fire-engine siren blared from the street.

'Now look what you've done!' the sergeant screamed at Ted.

'I haven't even started,' Ted shouted back. He yelled at his family above the noise. 'OK, everyone, listen to me. We have to go home and pack our bags. We're flying tonight.'

'My piano prize!' said Suzie.

'My pink petunias!' said Clare.

'My poor Pucker!' cried JP.

'Poor Pucker precisely,' said Ted. 'The Powers are going to Paris!'

4

Prisoners in Petersburg

The concrete floor of the cage was covered in straw. A bowl of dirty water sat beside the locked cage door, along with the remains of the day's single meal – stale breadcrumbs and an old bone. Pucker lay with his head propped on his front paws, watching Penelope in the cage opposite, his heart going pitter-patter.

At the entrance to the long prison room sat a guard with a truncheon stuck in his belt, reading a newspaper with funny-looking letters on it. Every few minutes he laughed to himself. But Penelope was crying softly. Along all sides of the room, disappearing into the cold shadows, were more cages and other jaildogs. Pucker already knew them well: Espike, a Guatemalan turkey-flusher with sleepy eyes and a tongue like a slab of corned beef. Butch from Texas, a chocolate birdhound with ears like slippers and a mournful howl. Mitzu the shitzu, who was jealous of Pucker's love and sniggered whenever Penelope started crying. Twin Afghan hounds named Axel and Lexa, who finished each other's sentences and had their own private language. And Hans, a miniature flugenshpugel with triangular teeth and no tail.

Pucker was *hurting*. Sore paws, sore neck, sore bum. The bumpy journey north had taken ten hours by plane, train and truck in that cramped, dark wooden box. And it was so cold.

He could hear the wind tearing at the prison roof and see the snow drifting against the single barred window at the end of the room. But sorest was his heart. His beloved was miserable and he was frustrated.

The question was, what was to be done? How were they going to escape this dreadful, desperate dungeon? The other dogs were OK, but they were so *wimpy*.

'You're in jail, pal,' Butch said when Pucker and Penelope had arrived the night before. 'Get used to it.'

'The Afghan embassy ...' Axel said, and Lexa finished, '... will get us out.'

'Oh, they might let *you* out,' Mitzu the shitzu said to Pucker, 'but *her*?' She narrowed her eyes and grinned at Penelope. *'Never.'*

And Espike? He slept. And slept. Waking every hour or so to sniff the bare bone or lick crumbs from the straw with his massive tongue before falling right back to sleep.

A clanking sound came from beyond the entrance. The guard looked up, threw his newspaper to the floor, and jumped to his feet,

straightening his truncheon. A low voice rumbled a command and the guard stepped aside. A long shadow fell across the prison floor, thick across the shoulders, with narrow hips and long thin legs.

The man walked in and Pucker shuddered. The man's eyes were evil. He was different from the guard and different from the dognapping painters. Better dressed but nastier. Much nastier.

'Look at them, Igor,' the man snarled in Russian. 'Stupid animals. Ugly, dumb creatures. A person must be very, very desperate to own such a lowly beast as a – *dog*.' He spat out this last word, disgusted. 'The only thing these pathetic fuzzballs have to recommend them is that their stupid owners are *filthy* rich.'

He laughed, and Pucker had never heard such a chilling sound. The man's clothes were all black and he wore lots of jewellery – gold chains and bracelets and chunky rings and a diamond earring that shone like the brightest star on the darkest night.

Of course *he* thought the dogs could understand nothing, but he didn't know – in fact, no-one knew, not even the Power family – that Pucker also had a super-power. *He could understand all languages,* human and doggie.

'Yes, filthy rich, except for this one,' the man said, rattling Pucker's cage. 'His owners are the Powers, who are stupid *and* penniless.'

Pucker growled.

'And isn't that bad luck for *him*?' the man said. 'Because money is the only thing keeping any of these miserable mongrels alive.'

Igor hitched at his belt and nodded rapidly. The man said to him, 'Did you telephone Prunella?'

'I did,' Igor said, 'yes, sir, I did. But there has been a change of plan.'

'What do you mean, change of plan?'

Igor pointed at Pucker. 'The owners of this manky mutt showed up at the meeting point in the Luxembourg Gardens.'

'The Powers?'

'Yes. So Prunella could not make contact with the Parfaits. Too risky.'

The man in black seemed to grow even larger. 'Too risky?' he shouted. 'Too *risky*! The Powers are the most incompetent family on the planet, you moron. So the ransom arrangements have not been made?'

'Ah .... no, Ivan Ivanov. I'm afraid not.'

In a rage, Ivan grabbed the truncheon from Igor's belt and cracked him over the head with it.

'I want that ransom, do you hear me?' Ivan snarled at Igor. 'Ten million euro, and not a cent less. I don't care if you have to *kill* the Powers.'

Pucker leapt at the man, howling fiercely and clutching the bars of the cage. Ivan shrank back in alarm. Then his eyes grew steely. Returning the truncheon to Igor, he said, 'Smack him.'

Igor blinded Pucker with pepper spray and gave him a couple of thwacks with the truncheon. But Pucker did not make a sound. He would not give these bullies the satisfaction. Besides, the real pain came not from the blows but from hearing Penelope whimper in fear. His poor darling! He had to get her out of this awful place.

Then Ivan grabbed Igor by the coat lapels. 'Listen to me, you peasant fool, I want a sample of this poodle's hair sent to Prunella in Paris.

Pronto. Tell her to bring it to the Parfaits. As proof. I don't care how many Powers there are. And if the hair isn't enough, we'll cut off a piece of her ear. Do you think you can do that?'

'Only a piece?' Igor said, laughing nervously.

'Shut up and do what you are told.'

Ivan threw Igor to the floor and stalked out of the room. Now all the dogs were howling in fright.

Panting with pain, still unable to see, Pucker lay in the straw. It was hard to believe that only twelve hours ago he had been capering in St Stephen's Green as he came across his perfect Penelope, his vision of beauty. From the peak of happiness to the pit of sorrow. It was true what they said – it is a dog's life.

But if life could go from good to bad so swiftly, then it could go back to good just as fast. If he would make it so.

So in his mind he promised Penelope he would prevent these repulsive reprobates from harming her precious poodle person, his prized pet.

So they thought he was a worthless dog from a penniless family, did they? Well, he was a Power. And Powers do not give up.

5

Prunella Appears

'*Joyeux anniversaire.*'

'What does that mean?' JP asked.

'What do you think it means?' Paulette said.

'Haven't a clue.'

JP and Paulette sat at the rear of the Pomeranian Café on Avenue Parmentier, drinking hot chocolate, while their parents had an intense discussion at a table near the door. The Powers had arrived in Paris that morning. Things were not going well, and the children had been told to sit near the back and behave themselves.

'Listen to me and say it,' Paulette said. *'Joyeux anniversaire.'*

'Oyovanajasair.'

She laughed. 'I thought you say you study French in school.'

'We haven't learned that word yet.'

'What word?' Suzie said, returning from the toilet.

Again Paulette said the phrase. *'Joyeux anniversaire.'*

'Oh,' Suzie said, pleased to be repeating something that would annoy JP, 'we've decided not to celebrate until after we get the dogs back.'

'My birthday – is that what you two are talking about?'

'I'm not talking about it,' Suzie said. 'For some reason, Paulette is wishing you a happy birthday.'

Paulette had been a lot nicer to him since the dognapping. And he liked her, but it was all sort of embarrassing with Suzie around. Especially when the two girls talked French. Like they were doing now. With lots of giggles.

'Stop that!' JP said.

'English for Dublin, French for Paris,' Paulette teased.

'It's not fair.'

'*Shhh,*' Suzie said suddenly, a finger to her lips. 'They're having a row.'

At the parents' table, Clare was saying to Ted, 'Just calm down.'

'I am calm,' Ted said, his head wrapped in a cloud of smoke. 'Whose side are you on, anyway?'

'There are no sides. We all want to get our doggies back.'

Ted pointed at Mr Parfait. 'Then tell him to stop blaming me. We had every right to be at the meeting this morning.'

Pierre Parfait looked a lot more tired than he had in Dublin, and his perfectly parted hair was not so perfect any more. He threw his hands in the air. 'My friend, do you not understand? The kidnappers, they say no police, no other people. They are watching the fountain, no? They are waiting to see me, only me, and you are there, snoofing around.'

'Snoofing?'

'Sniffing, snooping, I don't know the words. I am French, not English.'

'We aren't English either. We're Irish.'

'But you speak English.'

'So do you.'

'Aaaaaaargh.'

'Your dad screams just like our dad,' JP whispered to Paulette.

Mrs Parfait said something snappy to Clare, and Clare talked back in French. Mrs Parfait spoke again. And Clare. And Mrs Parfait. The voices got louder with every phrase. And though JP couldn't understand a word, he knew it wasn't a happy conversation. His mum's face clouded over. Then the sky clouded over and the café grew dark. Their mum was getting more like their dad every day – when she was angry her power to control the weather got out of control.

'Not now, Mum,' Suzie said under her breath.

But Clare was standing up and her face was red. *'Non!'* she shouted, and the café windows flashed with lightning and were flooded with water, as if someone was spraying them with a power hose.

JP looked at Suzie. But she had her head down and was pressing her fingers to her temples.

Whhsssshht. At that, the sky cleared and the café windows were glittering with sunshine.

'Yay!' the children shouted.

The Power and Parfait parents appeared stunned and seemed to forget that they were fighting. And the other people in the café resumed their chattering and everything was OK again.

Until ...

Total silence. A sudden atmosphere of gloom. And doom. But it wasn't the weather this time. Standing at the café entrance was a woman so scary looking that JP felt his stomach flip.

'Oh my God,' Suzie whispered. 'Prunella D Mon.'

'Who?'

Suzie did not reply. Prunella was dripping

wet, from her lizard-skin boots to her zebra striped skirt to her gloves trimmed with fox fur to her cape with black spots. She took a soaked handkerchief from her mink purse and slowly wiped her face. Her long black hair, streaked with gray, was plastered to her head, and she had a face on her like a dirty dishcloth.

'I suppose you all think that's very funny,' she said to the parents in an English accent, dropping the handkerchief to the floor with a plop. 'What makes me think the Powers made it rain on me *on purpose?*'

She stared at Clare fiercely with eyes as red as burning coals.

'She's so cruel,' JP whispered to Suzie.

'I heard that,' Prunella shrieked, pointing a painted finger at JP. 'Don't you *dare* criticise *me*, you silly little Irish flyboy.'

Later, Suzie would explain it all to JP: how Prunella had been a big fan of Cruella de Vil, an evil rich woman who kidnapped Dalmatian puppies for their fur. And Prunella had learned evil ways from her. JP could see it in her smouldering eyes and in the long, quivering finger.

He felt like a butterfly pinned to a board. What was he to say? What was he to do?

His mother came to his rescue, stepping between him and Prunella.

'How dare you talk to my son like that!' she said.

Prunella took a step back. But a wicked smile slowly spread across her face.

'Oh, I see. The Power *family*. All for one and one for all. But there's just one tiny little problem, isn't there? One tiny *furry* problem. A member of your wonderful, powerful family is missing, isn't he? And who do you think is the only person in this big, bad, dog-eat-dog world who can get him back for you? Who?'

Ted and the Parfaits stood up and joined Clare

'Oh, I have the attention of all of you now, don't I?'

Prunella reached into her pocket and took out a tuft of curly poodle hair, wrapped in a familiar pink ribbon.

Paulette shrieked and fainted into JP's arms.

'Where's Penelope?' Patricia Parfait cried. 'What have you done to my daughter's darling?'

'Done to her?' Prunella said, twirling the

ribbon on her little finger. 'Why, nothing, my dear. Nothing at all. I would never lay a finger on your delightful little doggie.' Her big smile collapsed into a ferocious scowl. 'But *Ivan* will!' she shouted, and then laughed so hard that her head shook and her skunk hair snapped back and forth like so many whips and drops of water fell from her head like a stormy wave splashing onto Sandymount Strand.

She cleared her throat and swept the dripping hair from her eyes. 'All of you, listen to me now and listen carefully. You had one chance this morning and you made a mess of that so I'm giving you a second chance. Ten million euro by Friday, do you understand? *Ten million*. And if you don't deliver it by noon, in unmarked fifty-euro notes, it won't be hair tied to this pink ribbon but something a little more ...*fleshy*.'

The families gasped.

'Why, you no-good –' Ted started to say, but Mr Parfait told him to shush and said to Prunella, 'Where do we bring the money?'

'All in good time, my good man, all in good

time. But one other thing,' she said, turning to Ted and Clare. 'One other condition. The Powers will suspend their super-powers for the next two weeks.'

'You can't do that,' Clare said.

'Oh no?'

'And if we don't?' Ted said.

Prunella pulled on her fur-lined gloves finger by finger, threw the corners of her cape over her shoulders and lifted her lip in a snarl. 'One more storm, one more fireball, one more pathetic attempt at flying by that pipsqueak son of yours, and I'll have the most elegant coat made from the pelts of Penelope – *and* Pucker.' Her face lit up in a huge, infernal smile. 'Oooo, the silky smoothness of pug fur and the woolly wonder of a poodle-fur collar. Wouldn't that look and feel simply *divine*?'

'How could anyone be so evil?' Clare murmured.

'Oh, I'm not evil. I just have good taste.'

6

Pucker's Plan

'Pssst. Penelope.'

Pucker spoke as quietly as he could so as not to wake Igor, who sat slumped in his chair. The brutal guard didn't speak Poodle or Pug, but he was quick to flash his truncheon if he heard doggie sounds of any description.

'*Oui, mon petit amour?*'

Pucker's heart pounded when he heard Penelope's poodley words and purring French accent. But he had to keep his head clear. So much was at stake.

'Ask Hans if he has finished the job,' Pucker whispered.

Penelope's cage was beside Hans's, which was beside Espike's, which was beside Butch's. On the opposite side of the row were Pucker, the Afghan twins, and Mitzu, propped in her cage like an Oriental queen. Using all his puggly charm, Pucker had convinced each to do a small job (except for Espike, who couldn't be counted on to stay awake).

Hans was to file one of the bars off using his sharp triangular teeth. ('They make a perfect saw,' Pucker had pointed out, which Hans had not noticed before.) Axel and Lexa had spent the day plucking long hairs from their shaggy coats and blowing them across to Mitzu and Penelope, who cleverly braided the hair into fine ropes, using tooth and nail, as Pucker had persuaded them they could do – and it turned out that he was right. They could! And Butch was told to be ready to howl.

'*Oui, cheri*. The job is done.'

There was no time to waste. Earlier that day, Pucker had overheard Igor and Ivan talking.

'Prunella just called,' Ivan had said. 'The fools have agreed to pay the money.'

'Horror-show,' said Igor. (Pucker knew that that meant 'good' in Russian, but it was *bad*.)

'We will be rich,' Ivan said, rubbing his hands together.

'And the dogs will live.'

'The dogs will what?'

Igor's voice grew nervous, the way it did when Ivan was about to slap him or grab him by the shirt and shake him until his teeth came loose. 'I mean, after we have the money, of course.'

'How did that putrid thought penetrate your pathetic little head?' Ivan asked.

'Uh ...' Igor stuttered, 'isn't that the deal?'

'The deal? *The deal?* Have I taught you nothing, Igor? You don't make deals with incompetents like the Powers. Or rich snobs like the

Parfaits. Give them half a chance and they'll string us up by the ankles and hang us from the top of the Eiffel Tower.'

'Oh, I see,' Igor said.

'Besides,' Ivan went on, 'do you think Prunella is in this for the money? She's the richest woman in England. Money means nothing to her. She wants that dog fur and she'll pay big time to get it. So we get the ten million ransom and she gives us another million when we've skinned those dumb beasts and delivered their coats. Think of it, Igor! I can buy that oil and gas company and build my mansion in Moscow and become a true tycoon.'

'You're a genius, Ivan.'

'Of course I'm a genius, you moron. Just keep your mouth shut in future and do what I tell you. And concentrate. We have work to do.'

Work to do! Igor was right, it was a horror-show, and Pucker was so frightened by what he had heard that he didn't dare tell the other doggie prisoners what was in store for them if his plan didn't work. News like that would make them so scared they wouldn't be able to move a muscle. And he needed them all to do exactly what he told them. He had thought the plan through to the tiniest detail. And explained to them, over and over, what each dog had to do.

'OK,' Pucker said. 'Is everyone ready?'

'Ruff.'

'Arf.'

'Bow-wow/wow-bow.'

'*Ja.*'

'Zzzzzz.'

Pucker took a deep breath. The timing had to be perfect. Everything had to happen just right.

'Now, Butch.'

'Arrrrooooooooooo.' Butch's howl was like a train whistle or a fire engine siren. Loud. And long.

Igor's snoozing head popped up like a jack-in-the-box. He fell off his chair and cursed a long string of *zhs* and *shchs*.

'Arrrrooooooooooo.'

Igor rubbed his eyes and fumbled for his truncheon. 'Quiet!' he screamed.

'Arrrrooooooooooo.'

Stumbling to his feet, Igor ran to Butch's

cage, the last one in the row. He rattled the bars with the truncheon. Butch's howl grew louder, longer, sharper.

'Silence, you hound,' Igor shouted, 'or I bonk you on your stupid skull!'

Butch, good old Butch, kept on howling.

Pucker nodded at Hans, who had cut one of the bars on his cage down to the last sliver of metal, so that it barely stayed in place. All Hans had to do now was nudge the bar and it would snap and fall to the floor, creating a gap just big enough for his tiny flugelshpugel body to fit through.

Igor had reached through the bars of Butch's cage and was swinging the truncheon like a Kilkenny hurler. Butch dodged the blows from side to side without stopping his thundering howl.

Hans punched out the bar and wiggled through the gap. Penelope and Mitzu had laid the ends of their ropes on the edge of their cages. Darting back and forth, Hans pulled the two rope ends to the middle of the space between the rows of cages and tied them together with his nimble little teeth. Then he ran to Igor's chair, hopped on the seat, and yapped and yapped, just as Butch stopped howling.

When Igor saw that Hans had escaped, he became even angrier and ran back towards his chair.

'Now!' Pucker shouted.

Penelope and Mitzu pulled on either end of the rope so that it tightened and rose, snagging Igor's foot and sending him sprawling. Hans was on Igor in a flash, plucking the keys from his belt and tossing them to Pucker before hopping onto Igor's head. While Igor thrashed about, trying to get this tailless little doggie off his face, Pucker used his other secret doggie super-power (key-turning) and unlocked his own cage and Alex and Lexa's. The big Afghans then pounced on Igor and held him on the floor. Pucker unlocked the rest of the cages and Mitzu and Penelope tied up Igor's legs and arms with the ropes. (They had got good at this tooth-and-nail business. Practice makes perfect.)

The chaos of it all! But it had worked perfectly. Pucker ran out of the prison to the front door of the building and nudged it open. It was dark outside, and so frosty that his breath billowed from his mouth in big clouds, and icicles hung like long knives from the low-hanging roof. A wide river, frozen solid and lit up by a giant moon, ran past the door. Across its great white space was a necklace of streetlamps, glittering in the cold. The road to freedom. And not a soul around.

He ran back to the prison room. 'C'mon everyone,' he hissed. 'The coast is clear.'

'You miserable mutts,' Igor shouted. 'I'll make you pay for this. I swear I will.'

'Oh, will you?' Butch said, giving him a big slobbery kiss.

'Aaargh!'

The dogs ran to the front door, waiting for Pucker to give them the all clear for their dash to freedom. He did a quick head count. One, two, three, four, five, six, seven. Seven? There were meant to be *eight*.

'Espike,' Butch cried. 'Where's Espike?'

Butch and Pucker returned and found

Espike asleep outside his cage, his tongue hanging from the side of his mouth like a huge slug, the loose sides of his mouth flapping as he snored.

'Espike, let's go! You can sleep later.'

The big lug struggled to his feet and followed them out. Together the gang of dogs ran out into the freezing cold and Pucker led them, single-file, onto the frozen river. Butch, who was last in line, shouted into the frosty night: 'Free at last, free at last, thanks to Puck-a-chuck we are free at last!'

7

President Proteo

The Parfaits lived in the Opéra neighbourhood of Paris, halfway between Pigalle and Palais Garnier. Their apartment was the penthouse of an old stone building that was decorated on the outside with fancy carvings and curly iron balconies.

The morning after Prunella's performance at the café, the Powers went to the Parfais' apartment to discuss the ransom. A tall man with a gray moustache and a funny hat opened the main door and led them inside. They entered an ancient lift with bars like a birdcage, a wooden floor and a petite padded piano stool perched beneath the push-buttons for the floors.

'The way I see it,' Ted Power said, as the lift creaked and groaned its way to the top of the building, 'you can't put a price on a pet. They're worth every penny we pay.'

'But, Ted,' Clare said, 'ten *million*?'

Ted lowered his voice. 'The Parfaits say they have the money.'

'But they can't be *that* rich.'

'If they're so rich,' JP said, 'how come they live in such a doken brown house?'

'You eejit,' Suzie said. 'It isn't broken down, it's *classical*.'

The lift shimmied to a halt and the family crossed the hall to the Parfaits' apartment door. Clare knocked the knocker, which was in the shape of a giant P.

Pierre Parfait opened the door. 'Ah, Power family, *bonjour, bienvenue*, please come in.'

A flat-faced fluffy Persian cat, with a twitchy nose and a white coat, squirmed in his arms. 'Be still, Don Mew,' Pierre said harshly.

Don Mew wore a necklace studded with sapphires. The precious stones were the precise colour of his piercing eyes, which had pinned JP.

'Why is the stat caring at me like that?' JP said.

As he often did when he was nervous, JP started floating. Suzie tugged him back to the floor just as the cat sprang from Pierre's arms, arched his back, and reached for JP with his claws extended.

'Mum!' JP shouted.

Clare clutched JP. Without even thinking about it, Suzie used telekinesis to stop Don Mew's paw in mid-air. Slowly, the cat slid backwards out of the room, as if pulled by an invisible string.

'Clare,' Ted said, 'was that you?'

'Of course not.'

'*Mon Dieu*,' Pierre said. 'Now is not that the strangest thing!'

Paulette walked in, looking puzzled. '*Le chat* –' she began, then noticed JP. '*Ah, bonjour,*' she said, and kissed him on both cheeks. He turned as red as a clown's nose. He was not having a good day.

'Is your mother home?' Clare asked.

'Oh, yes, Madame Power,' Paulette said, 'but *maman*, she is not feeling very well.'

'Oh, dear.'

'She will be fine,' Pierre said. 'Don't worry about her. We have good news. There is a special guest in the *salon* I would like you to meet.'

'But we're here to talk about the dognapping,' Ted said, 'not waste time drinking hot chocolate and making tall talk.'

'No, no, no,' Pierre said. 'No tall talk. I have for you a man with a *plan*.'

He led them through the apartment, which was filled with priceless antiques and expensive paintings and polished rugby trophies, until they reached a bright room at the rear with huge picture windows that looked down on the pathways of Paris.

And there, gazing out the window, hands

clasped behind his back, was – the president of Russia!

'I am pleased to present President Pluto,' Pierre said.

The Powers were amazed. He looked just like he did on television, except he was shorter. And he had put a shirt on.

The president bowed and spoke briefly in Russian.

'I will translate,' Pierre Parfait said with a sly smile. He was not acting like a man whose daughter's beloved pet was being held by blood-thirsty criminals. 'I know, how you say, many languages.' He cleared his throat. 'The president, he says he has heard that Russian criminals are responsible for the kidnapping of our precious pets, and he will do everything in his power to rescue them. In fact, he guarantees it.'

Ted stepped forward and put on his serious-dad face. 'May I say, Mr President, on behalf of all my family, that we are all as pleased as pretty pink punch to know that you are working hard to free our little Puck-a-stuck.'

President Pluto laughed. 'Pook-a-stook?'

'Well, that's what we like to call him.'

'What a silly name!' the president said in squeaky English. 'A silly, silly name. And you, sir, you are a silly-looking man with smoke coming out of your ears.'

The president's voice rose and dipped and his face turned rubbery and his arms and legs stretched and his clothes changed fabric and colour. Within seconds he was completely transformed: before them stood a tall, thin, sharp-boned man, with a wrinkled face and bug eyes and a chin that came to a point. He wore fire-engine-red one-piece overalls, black runners and a red cap with little silver wings on the side. Around his neck was a chain dangling a big silver P.

Mr Parfait was about to say something when Ted shouted, 'Proteo!'

'Yes, Power, it is I.'

'You no-good shape-shifter,' snarled Ted. 'How did you get here?'

Proteo stuck his nose in the air. 'I was invited.'

'Invited!' Ted was steaming, his collar crackling and his cuffs spilling sparks.

'Yes!' said Proteo. 'Mr Parfait here found me in the superhero supplement to the *Magic Times*.'

'You know each other?' Pierre said.

Clare stepped forward. Thunder clouds suddenly pressed against the picture windows so that the streets below disappeared. Lightning sizzled. 'Know each other?' Clare said. 'I should say we do. Proteo cast the deciding vote when the International Superhero Association suspended us.'

Proteo was a Canadian superhero who could take the shape and sound of any living creature. But he was also known for turning friends into enemies and enemies into money. He had a sweet tooth and would sell out his grandmother for a bar of chocolate.

'What can I say?' Proteo said with a shrug. 'You Powers – you are a disaster waiting to happen.'

'And you are a liar and a rogue!' Ted shouted. A small fireball leapt from Ted's fingers and fell on the shaggy white rug. Mr Parfait stamped it out.

'Pffff,' Proteo said. 'See what I mean? Even

when you are forbidden to use your powers, you have no control. Who knocked the head off the Statue of Liberty when you were trying to rescue the Gotham mayor's daughter? Who made the hands of Big Ben go backwards? Who tried to rescue the earthquake orphans in San Francisco and caused another earthquake?'

'This is outrageous,' Ted cried. 'You are insulting me and my family.'

With both hands sparking, Ted reached for Proteo's neck, but Pierre Parfait jumped between them.

'*Un moment*, Mr Power, *un moment*. Mr Proteo is our friend. He is here to help. And he has a plan.'

'I wouldn't trust any plan this chancer has,' Ted shouted. 'C'mon, kids, we're leaving.'

'But, Dad,' Suzie said, 'what about Pucker?'

'Mr Power,' Pierre said, 'please listen. Our friend here, he is a genius.'

Proteo stuck out his lower lip. 'I am not speaking to this buffoon,' he said.

'*Me* – a buffoon?' Ted said, turning to Pierre. 'Look at his uniform. Does he look like a serious superhero to you?'

Pierre grew cross. 'Mr Power and Mr Proteo, *if you please*. We are all in this together.'

'Dad, we have to save Pucker. And Penelope.'

Ted crossed his arms and stared at the smouldering carpet like a sulking child. 'OK, OK, I'll listen.'

Proteo started speaking like a very important person. 'The dognappers,' he said, 'they will accept the ransom only from Mr Parfait.'

'We *know* that,' Ted said.

'And Mr Parfait will deliver the money, ten million, as arranged with the wicked Prunella D Mon – tomorrow at noon in front of the Eiffel Tower.'

'How do we know –'

'Except,' Proteo interrupted, raising a finger, 'it won't be real money. And it won't be the real Mr Parfait either.'

Pierre Parfait spoke, all excited: 'You see – this is genius, don't you know – the money will be Monopoly money, and it will be Proteo delivering it in the *shape* of me. He will hand over the fake money and then change himself into a terrifying beast. The evil men, they will run

away like little piggies, run run run, and we will have our pooches back.'

The Powers stared at him.

'That's the maddest plan I ever heard,' Ted said.

'Why, thank you.'

'No. I mean *mad*. It will never work.'

Proteo pointed at Ted. 'He is just jealous because he cannot use his powers. And it's lucky he can't, because if he did he would *burn those doggies alive*.'

Ted lunged again, but Proteo turned into a butterfly and flitted about the room. The place was now full of the smoke streaming from Ted's ears and armpits. He was chasing the butterfly, trying to snag it with his hands. Don Mew had returned and leapt onto JP and sunk his claws into his trousers so that JP screamed and Paulette tried to pull the cat off him and Clare was waving smoke away and Pierre was holding Ted back and …

It was chaos. Typical Powers chaos. And it took Suzie several minutes of secret telekinesis, reverse weather and thought control to sort it all out.

But now her dad had *really* had enough. 'I'm leaving,' he said. 'We're all leaving. Enough of this nonsense.'

He marched his family to the front door. Pierre and Paulette trailed behind, pleading with them to stay. Don Mew lurked in the hallway and JP was so nervous he was floating four feet off the ground.

'Don't worry,' Suzie whispered to Paulette. 'Everything will be all right. I promise.'

But Ted was not all right. As he slammed shut the lift door, he shouted at Pierre Parfait through the bars. 'You think that's a plan? It's a pig's dinner is what it is. And Proteo is as mad as a platter. *We'll* show you a plan. The Powers will prevail.'

As the lift grumbled downwards Mr Parfait leaned over the railing and shouted, 'No, you must not use your powers. Please. If you do, *zey will kill ze doggies!*'

8

Pinched at the Palace

Meanwhile, back in St Petersburg, the dogs raced across the frozen river. Pucker and Penelope led the gang, with Butch at the rear, making sure Espike did not fall asleep. Moonlight glistened on the ice and the stars in the black winter sky shone like drops of liquid silver.

They had to keep moving. By now Igor would have escaped from the braided ropes and raised the alarm. He and Ivan would be after them. Soon.

Plus, it was cold. Really cold. Pucker knew if they didn't keep running they'd get frostbite on their doggie noses and bare doggie paws. As they ran he gazed lovingly at Penelope. She had had chunks of her hair cut off by those beastly men but she looked as beautiful as ever.

On the other side of the river was a motorway. The gang waited until traffic was light and loped across. They scrambled up a snowy hill and stopped at the edge of a huge public garden to catch their breath.

'I'm cold,' said Mitzu.

'I'm hungry,' said Hans.

'We're scared,' said Axel and Lexa.

'Zzzzzz,' said Espike.

Butch was staring back at the river. 'Uh-oh,' he said. 'Here comes trouble.'

Ivan and Igor, wearing snow shoes and carrying shotguns, were scooting across the ice and catching up on them fast.

The dogs ducked into the garden, running between the dark plants and trees without any idea of where they were headed. Behind them were shouts. Then gunshot. Pucker and Penelope were breathing hard. With their little legs, Mitzu and Hans could not keep up, so they climbed onto Axel and Lexa, clutching the Afghans' long hair and riding like jockeys. Somehow Espike managed to plod along, and Butch gave directions from the back of the pack.

'Keep your heads down. Go to the left. To the right. Faster, doggies, faster!'

They passed broken-down greenhouses and frozen fountains and statues of naked humans wearing caps of crusty snow. Ahead, streetlamps shone in the gloom. They bounded towards the light, huffing and puffing, snow flying from their heels.

Then, bang! Pucker hit a fence. A tall wire fence. Too high to climb and no gaps that even the smallest of them could squeeze through.

To the right and left were tangles of plants and trees so thick it was like walls on both sides. They were in a cul-de-sac.

The dogs piled into each other at the base of the fence, whimpering. Behind them, Ivan and Igor's shouts grew louder.

'What do we do now, Pucker?' Butch said. 'They have *guns*.'

Pucker peered through the diamond shapes of the wire. The lights ahead, he saw now, came from a beautiful palace, with gleaming white columns and golden domes and tall, glittering windows. Getting to that palace, he thought, would be like getting to heaven. They would be safe. They would be warm. They would be happy.

But it was hopeless. The fence was too high and too sturdy, and there was no way out but back into the hands of the vicious criminals.

'I know!' Penelope shouted.

She turned to Hans. *'Du! Grabe!'* she said to him.

'What's she saying?' Butch yelled.

Pucker, who understood German as he did

every language, said, 'Brilliant! She told him to dig.'

Hans went to work like a tiny JCB, burrowing into the earth beneath the fence. It didn't matter that the ground was frozen and covered with snow. His tiny triangular teeth worked like a buzz-saw, digging deep and digging quick, sending a spray of dirt and ice into the air behind him.

Ivan and Igor were now less than a hundred metres away, and the curse words were *shch*-ing and blinding from their lips like an avalanche.

'Hurry, Hans, hurry,' Pucker cried.

Soon the tunnel beneath the fence was big enough for Mitzu, then Penelope, then Butch. They squeezed through. The bad men were now less than fifty metres away. Hans dug more. Axel and Lexa, long and thin as they were, made it to the other side. But the hole still wasn't big enough for Espike.

Espike wasn't scared. In fact, he could barely keep his eyes open. 'You escape,' he said lazily to Hans and Pucker, 'I will estay here.'

'Never!' Pucker said. 'All for one and one for all.'

Twenty-five metres. Twenty. Hans dug faster and faster, whirling like a hamster on a wheel while bullets and bad words whizzed past his head.

Finally the hole was big enough for Espike.

'Let's go,' Pucker said.

Hans ran through and Espike lumbered into the hole. But he got stuck! So Pucker pushed and pushed from behind while Butch pulled Espike by the tongue from the front and Ivan and Igor were five meters away and ... *pllff*! Espike popped through with Pucker hustling after him as Ivan's big hand reached into the hole and grabbed Pucker's curly puggly tail and the tail stretched and stretched and slithered out of Ivan's grubby grasp and the dogs capered through the snow, running towards the palace and barking for joy.

'*Whew!*' Pucker thought in five different languages.

The bad guys must have been out of bullets because there was no more gunfire. The doggies ran into a large square in front of the palace, which had been swept clear of snow. A few policeman stood at the edge of the square, but they didn't seem to notice the dogs.

Back at the fence, Ivan and Igor had climbed over and were heading towards the square – walking slowly towards the policemen. The square was as big as a football pitch and there was no place to run, no place to hide. Pucker led the gang to the palace entrance, where three arched doorways led to a brightly lit hallway.

But as the pooches were looking longingly at the warm room, a palace guard in a red uniform and huge furry hat stepped in front of them.

'*Nyet, nyet, nyet,*' he said, shaking his finger. They didn't need a translation. They knew what he meant. No.

Pucker looked back at the bad guys. They were talking to a policeman and pointing at the dogs. The policeman nodded and started walking towards them.

Not again!

Pucker said to Butch, '*Now* what are we going to do?'

Butch winked at him. 'I have an idea.'

Butch walked over to an empty flower pot, threw

back his head and howled: 'Arrrrooooooooooooo.'

The guard shouted at Butch, 'You over there, that's enough of that howling.'

'Arf,' Butch said, lifted his leg and whizzed into the pot.

The guard nearly had a canary, his face turning as red as his uniform. He ripped off his hat, threw it on the ground, and ran after Butch. But Butch was an experienced birdhound who had spent his early life chasing poopbirds in the swamps of east Texas. He was light on his paws and easily danced away from the flustered guard. Meanwhile, the other dogs slipped into the palace. Oh, it was so bright, so colourful, so warm! And so many places to hide!

'Follow me,' Pucker shouted, and led them up a wide staircase. Butch darted between the legs of the guard, who spun like a top and fell to the ground while Butch scampered after his friends.

The dogs found themselves in a large room with a polished marble floor, a high ceiling and a shimmering chandelier with hundreds of tiny light bulbs. The heat was wonderful. The walls were covered with velvet drapes and dozens of old paintings. And almost every painting had a dog in it. There were birdhounds and terriers and bulldogs and setters. Spaniels and mastiffs and retrievers and wolfhounds. Dogs chasing foxes and swimming in rivers. Dogs lying in the sun and sleeping by the fire.

Pucker's gang yapped and clapped and flapped their ears. Five minutes ago they had been frozen and fearful. Now, here they were, toasty and together and in a doggie museum!

Penelope nudged Pucker. 'We must keep going.'

'Uh, listen everybody,' Pucker said to the others. His pug forehead was even more wrinkled than usual. 'We should keep moving. We should find a small room that is out of the way where we can hide and scout for food and think about what we are going to do next.'

But the dogs weren't listening. Axel and Lexa had found a painting of twin Afghans sitting beside a camel. Butch was gazing lovingly at a female Scottish birdhound in a tartan jacket. Espike was snoozing, paws in the air. Mitzu and Hans bickered over a painting called 'Lady with Lapdog'. Was the lady's dog a shitzu or a flugenshpugel?

It didn't matter, Pucker wanted to say, it's not *important*. But the mutts ignored him. They were in another world. Penelope was the only one who understood. With Pucker she ran from one dog to the other, trying to get them to leave this room and find a place where they could –

Click.

Oh, that was not a good sound. Not a good sound at all.

'Nobody move.'

It was Ivan. And Igor. Pointing shotguns at them. While behind them came the guard and the policemen with cages.

Pucker pleaded. Penelope prayed. Espike eslept. But it was no use. The pups were pinched.

9

The Payoff

Suzie lay on her bed in the Powers' hotel room, trying to read. So trying to read. Paulette had given her a French translation of *The Dark Knight* and she was working her way through it slowly. Very slowly. Because beside her was JP, sniffling and snorting and biting his trembling lower lip as he held back the tears.

He was so sad. He had found a family photo album on Ted's tablet and was clicking through doggie pictures and trying not to cry.

The day they brought Pucker home from the shelter, his little face scrunched up like a baby's.

Sigh.

His graduation picture from the Perfect Pug Puppy training academy.

Sniffle.

The time he won the ugliest dog competition at the Ballybrickhead Dog and Pony Show.

Boo-hoo-hoo.

And on her other side were her mum and dad, staring out the hotel window at the Eiffel Tower, *tsking* and *hmmffing* and *grrring*.

'He'll make a mess of it,' Ted said.

'Of course he will,' Clare said. 'What else would you expect from –' she made a face – '*Proteo*.' When she said the name it sounded like she was spitting.

Suzie checked the time. It was nearly noon, when Proteo was meant to meet the dognappers, hand them the Monopoly money and do his tricks.

Ted pointed at the grassy park in front of the tower. 'There, right down there. That's where it's all going to happen. And we can't do a thing.'

Clare stood beside him. 'Our hands are tied,' she said. 'Our wings are clipped. Our powers are powerless.'

'*Mum,*' Suzie said. 'I'm *trying* to read.'

'How can you read at a time like this?'

'I don't think you should even be looking at the tower,' Suzie said. 'We're not meant to be anywhere near by when it happens.'

'We're not near by,' Ted said, 'we're far by.'

'But what if they see us?'

'Look, Suzie,' JP said, pointing at a snap of Pucker howling at the front door of their house in Castlerock. In the distance was the post-man, running for his life. The footpath was scattered with packages and letters. ''Member this – when he pooed the chostman's trousers?'

'Yes. And dad took a picture of it.'

'Poor little Stuck-a-puck. We have to get him back, Suzie. We have to.'

Waaahhhhh.

'I know, JP. I know.'

'There she is!' Ted shouted.

The children ran to the window. Far below they saw Prunella D Mon walking across the grassy park leading to the foot of the Eiffel Tower. Behind her were two large men in black, each carrying something heavy.

'Who are they?' Clare said. 'And what are they carrying?'

On the opposite side of the park, walking towards Prunella and her evil assistants, was Pierre Parfait (actually Proteo in the *shape* of Pierre) clutching a black briefcase.

'They look so tiny,' Ted said.

'My skeletope!' JP shouted, and ran to his suitcase.

But he was so nervous he couldn't hold the telescope to his eye, so Suzie took it from him, looked through it and saw Prunella, dressed head to foot in animal skins, and the two men with her.

'Wooden boxes,' she said. 'They're carrying two wooden boxes.'

'The booden woxes,' JP said. 'That's where they keep the doggies! It's Pucker and

Pepellone – they're going to be saved.'

JP was so excited he was floating.

'Let me see,' Ted said, grabbing the telescope.

There was smoke inside the room and storm clouds outside.

'Mum, stop the weather or Prunella will know we're here,' said Suzie.

'I can't help it,' said Clare.

Ted started trembling. 'The *fool*.'

'What, Dad, what?'

'He's *not* giving them the money.'

'But it's fake anyway, so –'

'I don't believe it! The men have grabbed Proteo. He won't let them have the briefcase. It's broken open. There's money everywhere, and – and ... *I can't see a thing*!'

Clare was so nervous she had created a monsoon. The rain was like a thick curtain. Suzie concentrated her full weather-reversal power and the rain stopped and the sun returned. And in the brightness they saw –

'Oh my!'

'What is he ...?'

'Cool!'

Proteo had turned himself into a dragon. And not just any dragon, but a massive fire-breathing monster with giant scaly wings and a long forked tongue and a tail as big as a dinosaur's. The briefcase had fallen to the ground and the money had been carried by the wind so that it was scattered all over the park, and loads of people (who had no idea it was fake) were running like mad around the grass picking up hundred-euro notes even though there were licks of flame from the dragon's mouth scorching the park benches and setting trees on fire.

'They're running away,' Ted shouted. 'The bad guys are running away.'

'Yippee!'

'And they've left the boxes behind.'

'Hurray!'

'And the boxes are ... the boxes are ... empty.'

Ted dropped the telescope. 'Those no-good, low-down, yellow-bellied lying dognappers. They were double-crossing us all along.'

'But we were double-crossing *them*,' Suzie said.

'But, Suzie, we're the *good* guys.' JP stood in the middle of the room. His hair stuck up at the back. He looked lost and lonely. 'So what happens now?'

'Now?' Ted looked at Clare. Clare looked at Ted. Suzie knew these looks. They meant trouble was coming. Trouble that pretended to be rescue.

'Proteo had his chance,' Clare said.

'And Proteo couldn't save the day,' Ted answered.

'So it falls on us.'

'To do our duty.' Ted turned to JP. 'Who are we, JP?'

'The Powers!' JP yelled.

'And what are we?'

'We're super.'

'Super what?'

'Pooper-*soured*!'

Ted leapt towards the door and Clare and JP charged after him.

'We're coming, Pucker,' shouted Ted.

'We'll save you,' yelled Clare.

'I have to go to the toilet,' screamed JP.

As they disappeared into the hall, Suzie said, 'Wait – we need a *plan*.'

Too late. They were gone.

Suzie sighed, closed her book and followed them out the door. It looked like she had work to do.

10

Pandemonium

Proteo stood in the plundered park looking perplexed. The earth around him was like a battlefield. But the mighty dragon who had laid waste the landscape had turned into a lanky, sleepy-headed, forgetful fella with torn clothes and not a spark of energy.

The Powers ran up to him.

'Proteo,' Clare called, 'which way did they go?'

'Which way did who go?'

'Prunella D Mon. The bad guys. Wake up!'

'I need to go back to the Parfaits' apartment.

I need a little – nap,' Proteo mumbled. 'You don't have any sweets, do you? Being a dragon really takes it out of me.'

Suzie's mum and dad looked at each other. It was their I-told-you-so look.

Pierre Parfait – the real Pierre Parfait – appeared breathlessly, with Paulette and a policeman.

Paulette saw the empty wooden boxes and wailed. *'Penelope, où est ma Penelope?'*

Suzie comforted her. JP looked up. Then pointed frantically. 'Mum, Dad – there they are!'

Climbing the stairs of the Eiffel Tower, her wild hair streaming behind her, was Prunella D Mon. Her evil henchmen were following her.

'Proteo,' Pierre pleaded, 'do something.'

Proteo raised a finger. 'I will, of course. But first I need a little sleep. And some pudding.' He lay on the grass and closed his eyes.

'Dad, c'mon,' JP yelled, 'let's get them!'

'Hold on, JP,' Ted said. 'Not so fast. We didn't get where we are today by acting like a pig in a pottery shop.'

Pierre stepped forward. 'May I introduce

Policeman Proust,' he said, indicating the man at his side. 'He will get ze doggies back.'

The policeman bowed.

'I'm sorry to disappoint you, Guard,' Ted said, 'but Mr Parfait has had his chance. This is the part of the story where the Powers take over. It is fate. It is who we are.' He pointed towards the tower. 'These evil-doers? We have them exactly where we want them.'

'What do you mean?' Pierre Parfait said.

'They are climbing up the tower. What are they going to do at the top?' Ted asked

'Why do you ask *me*?' said Pierre Parfait.

'I mean to say,' Ted said, 'we have them trapped. When they get up there, they have nowhere to go.' He stretched out his hands and smiled. He had it all worked out.

Again JP pointed at the sky. 'Dad, look!'

A helicopter hovered near the peak of the Eiffel Tower like a giant insect. Ted looked confused.

'The helicopter is their rescue plan,' Suzie cried. 'They're going to get away!'

Clare stepped forward. 'JP,' she said, 'take your cape. Fly up there and keep an eye on the helicopter. And make sure your mobile phone is on. Ted, you follow Prunella up the tower. Quickly!'

'What are you talking about, Clare?' Ted protested. 'We need a plan.'

'Ted, this *is* a plan,' said Clare. 'Listen to me for once.'

'I always listen to you.'

'Good,' said Clare. 'Then bring this French policeman with you. Up the tower. I'll create some wind and fog, so Prunella and those big goons she's with can't see where they're going, and you and Policeman Proust can arrest them.'

'I don't know, Clare, I –'

'Ted!'

Ted ran towards the tower, grumbling. Policeman Proust followed, several sets of handcuffs jangling on his belt.

'JP,' Clare cried, 'what are you waiting for? *Go!'*

JP took off, knocking over a cart selling ice creams, bashing into a kissing couple and upsetting a baby stroller, which spilled two crying toddlers onto the burnt grass.

'Suzie,' Clare said, 'you are command central.

Stay in touch with Dad and JP with your phone. Just because you don't have super-powers doesn't mean that you can't help out.'

For the one million and thirty-third time in her life, Suzie rolled her eyes. 'Yes, Mum.'

Clare went off to be by herself so she could concentrate on the weather. Proteo snoozed on the lawn. It was a good plan. Her mum had worked it all out. Quickly. So why was Suzie sure that it wouldn't work? Because the Powers' plans never worked.

Her dad would blow something up, or JP would fly through a skyscraper window, or her mum's lightning would cause a power outage. And Suzie – Suzie would, as usual, have to save the day. And pretend it was her family who had done it.

And where were the dogs? The Powers could capture Prunella, but would she tell them where Pucker and Penelope were imprisoned? Or would the family be back where they started?

So Suzie peered up at the tower and turned on her super-vision.

A growing wind began to blow wisps of fog

through the tower's big beams. JP, for once, was flying in a straight line, his green and red cape rippling in the wind like the Italian flag. Ted and the policeman were bounding up the steps two at a time. And Prunella and her boys had reached the tower's first level and entered one of the lifts that took people to the top.

'So,' Suzie said beneath her breath, her X-ray sight piercing the lift's metal door so that she could see Prunella's evil face, 'you want to make a coat out of Pucker and Penelope, do you? We'll see about that.'

She concentrated. If she could make objects move she could also make them stop. The lift groaned to a halt.

Suzie listened in with her super-hearing.

'What is going on?' Prunella snapped at the two men. 'Why aren't we moving?'

They shrugged.

'You stupid, stupid men,' Prunella complained. 'I thought you had all this arranged. First, there is this monstrous dragon. Then the money blows away. And now we're stuck in this lift while Ivan waits in the helicopter. What do you think he's going to say when he finds out we don't have the ten million? He won't be happy. But I'll tell you one thing – I want the fur of those doggies and I want it today. Do you hear me? I've kept *my* end of the bargain.'

The fog grew thicker. JP was circling the helicopter, getting too close to the swirling blades. Suzie rang him. He didn't hear the phone. Then she rang her dad, who had just reached the first level of the tower.

'Dad, listen to me,' Suzie ordered. 'Prunella is in lift number one. On her way to the top. Take lift number two.'

'Suzie, stop distracting me. The lifts are broken.' Ted was out of breath.

'No, Dad – it's only the first lift. Lift two is fine.'

'How do you know all this?'

'Mum told me,' Suzie said, fibbing.

'OK, I'm on my way.'

Suzie ran to her mum, who was sitting on the grass with her hands on her temples and her eyes squeezed shut.

'Leave me alone, Suzie,' Clare said.

'Mum, you have to stop the weather. Dad's going to catch Prunella at the top.'

'I know. That's what I told him to do.'

'No – I mean, he has her trapped. But you have to get rid of the fog or he won't be able to see what he is doing.'

'How do you know all this?' Clare asked.

'Dad told me,' Suzie said, fibbing again.

'OK, then.' Clare went into reverse-weather mode.

Suzie looked up. When her dad was nearly at the top of the tower, she let Prunella's lift start moving again.

But the fog was getting worse. And the wind blew harder.

'Mum, what are you *doing*?'

'I don't know. I –'

The wind blew JP closer to the helicopter and the blades snagged his cape. Suzie gasped as she watched him whirl round and round, at hundreds of kilometres an hour, until his cape tore and he went whizzing across the Paris sky like a shot off a shovel.

'JP!' Suzie screamed.

In the meantime, Ted and the policeman had got lost in the fog.

Prunella ran from the lift, just as the helicopter dropped a rope ladder to the platform below. She scampered up the ladder, stopping just long enough to kick the first of her assistants in the head. He fell on top of the other man and they both tumbled back onto the platform, where the policeman had emerged from the fog in time to snap them both into handcuffs.

But Prunella had escaped. Even without super-hearing, Suzie could hear her evil laugh piercing the fog as the helicopter turned in the sky.

Off it flew. While Suzie looked on helplessly.

Now what was going to happen?

And where was JP?

11

The Poo Pit

Ducks quacked. Hens clucked. Pigs oinked.
  In French.
  The day dawned. Pucker lay in his wooden box, his little prison, listening to the farmyard sounds. Was he in France? Why had they been brought here?

From the Petersburg palace the dogs had been whisked on to the back of a truck. All night they had bumped along, each of the dogs in his own box. But they were still together. Pucker had heard Mitzu crying, Butch howling, Espike esnoring. The truck had stopped and the boxes were moved into a big room, and all night Pucker had lain awake, listening in the dark.

Until now. The morning. A rustle outside.

Pucker peered through one of the holes in the box and saw the legs of their guard. And heard a voice – Igor's voice – talking to himself in Russian: 'Not long now. Like Ivan says, keep them alive. Keep them healthy. And then we get the big money from Prunella.'

Pucker's blood ran icy. So he was finally going to meet the evil Prunella D Mon. No name struck more terror into the heart of a pooch. Every dog on the planet knew what would happen if they fell into the deadly clutches of de Vils or Mons.

Poodle pullovers.

Pug pants.

Afghan afghans.

They needed to be saved.

But where were the Powers?

High above the French countryside, the helicopter chopped along. Ivan was at the controls. He was not in a good mood.

'I *told* you to get the money first,' he said to Prunella.

'Well, you should have told those bumbling bumpkins you sent with me. Never in my life have I met two more incompetent nincompoops. They couldn't even climb the ladder into the helicopter without slipping and falling. They're probably telling the police *everything* right now.'

'Aaaaargh.'

'There's no point screaming, Ivan. You can kiss that ten million good-bye.'

'Those morons.'

'Of course.' Her voice trailed away.

'Of course what?' Ivan said.

'Of course you'll still have my money. A million euro – for all the dogs.'

'We agreed a million for the poodle and the pug. Not the rest of them.'

'I want them all,' Prunella shouted. 'Every one. I have plans for my wardrobe, *big* plans.'

'Then you are going to have to come up with more money. Millions more.'

'You're as greedy as the rest of them,' Prunella said. 'I've a good mind to –' Her face froze in disgust.

'What's wrong?' Ivan said.

Prunella pointed one of her long painted fingers at the window. Flying alongside the helicopter was JP.

'Who is that?' Ivan asked.

'*That*,' Prunella said, 'is the pathetic little pipsqueak son of the Powers. Sp g for his parents, no doubt.'

'The Powers? Here, take o he controls.'

Ivan got his shotgun fro the rear of the cockpit, slid open the side wi dow, and took careful aim.

'It's ringing, Mum,' Suzie said.

'Why isn't he answering?'

'Because he's *flying*.'

'He's so inconsiderate.'

'Wait a minute. JP, JP, is that you?'

JP's excited squeaky voice sounded in Suzie's ear. 'I'm following them, Suzie. I'm flying right beside their helicopter.'

'Be careful, JP.'

'Don't worry, I'm –'

KABLOOM. Silence.

✦

'Penelope, can you hear me?' Pucker called.

'Oui, mon cheri.'

Pucker spoke to his beloved through the hole in the box. He kept his voice as quiet as he could. 'We have to get out of here. We need another plan.'

'What do you sink?'

'Sink? Oh, *think*. I don't know. We are in France. Maybe you can get the farmyard animals to help us.'

A deep laugh filled the barn. It was Igor.

'Listen to them growl,' he said out loud. 'Do they think they can fool me like last time?'

From the sky came a whining sound.

'This time,' Igor continued, 'that nasty little flugenshpugel is in a solid steel box. This time those ugly Afghans have had their hair shaved. And that birdhound? He can howl his head off and I won't listen.'

The whining sound grew louder. Igor went to the barn door and looked up.

'What the –?' he said.

The whine came closer. And closer.

JP came zipping out of the sky like a falling star. Igor didn't see him until it was too late. *POW!* JP crashed to earth right on top of Igor, knocking him out cold.

And JP? Igor's fat body was like a big pillow. The boy was fine.

✦

The Powers were panic-stricken. The Parfaits were perturbed. Paulette prayed.

What had happened to JP?

The two families stood on top of the Eiffel

97

Tower, petrified. Perplexed. Suzie stood stock-still, the phone in her hand.

'Was that a gunshot?' Ted asked Suzie. 'It sounded like a gunshot.'

'I don't know, Dad.'

'Then why did the phone go dead?'

'Don't say "dead",' Clare said. 'Please don't.'

'Where is JP,' Paulette wailed. 'What are we going to do?'

'*Excusez-moi*,' Policeman Proust said to the Powers.

'Not now,' Pierre Parfait said to the policeman.

'But –'

'Not now, *monsieur*. Can't you see these good people are worried about their son?'

'The phone,' Proust said.

'The phone, yes, yes, we know about the phone.'

'Wait a minute,' Ted said. 'Let's hear what the man has to say.'

The policeman spoke to Pierre in French.

'But of course,' Pierre said, his eyes lighting up. 'The police can track PJ –'

'JP.'

'Yes. JP. Zey can track him by his mobile phone.'

＊

Outside the barn, the helicopter roared as it touched down in the farmyard. Geese and ducks scattered in the wind from the blades, feathers flying.

Ivan jumped out.

'Aren't you going to help me down?' Prunella said to Ivan.

'Get down yourself.'

'And you call yourself a gentleman,' Prunella said.

But Ivan wasn't listening. The blades had stopped and the farmyard was quiet.

'Where is Igor?' he asked.

Ivan couldn't see him, but Igor was at the back of the barn. Tied up. A handkerchief stuffed in his mouth so he couldn't make a sound. JP was standing guard. He had unlocked the doggies from their boxes.

And Penelope had come up with a plan.

'Igor,' Ivan shouted.

He looked at the barn suspiciously. After a few moments he returned to the helicopter and got his shotgun.

'I don't care if you kill those beasts,' Prunella shouted, 'but I don't want a single hair of their perfect pelts destroyed. Do you hear me? Otherwise you won't get a penny out of me.'

'*Shhh.*'

Slowly, Ivan crept close to the barn door, gun raised. He stopped. Listened carefully.

'Igor?' he said. No answer. 'Igor!'

From behind the helicopter came a small bark. Penelope's bark. Ivan whirled and took aim. But he couldn't see Penelope, who had hidden in the henhouse. She barked again. He ran towards the henhouse.

But she wasn't barking. She was speaking chicken French. 'He has a gun, my little chickadees, beware, he has a gun!'

When the chickens heard this they panicked and burst from the henhouse door just as Ivan was about to open it. A massive rush of clucking, clawing chickens hit him in the face so that he dropped the gun and thrashed his arms as he tried to escape from the scratching and feathery flapping. From behind the barn Hans and Butch and the shaven Afghans came running, ready with ropes and chains and locks to knock Ivan over and tie him up. They knew what they were doing. They had done it before.

Prunella, seeing this disaster unfold, jumped from the back of the helicopter and ran towards the road. But Pucker was alert. He sprinted after her, his little legs pumping like pistons. Down the road he raced, watching Prunella in her zebra skirt and lizard-skin shoes ahead of him. Slowly he made up ground. She hopped over a fence and dashed through a meadow, but Pucker was right behind her now, snapping at her heels. Ahead was a concrete circle – a slurry pit where the farmer collected all the poo of the cows and sheep and pigs. Pucker saw it, smiled and barked rapidly.

Prunella turned to see how close he was. Pucker had slowed down, pretending he was tired. Prunella threw back her head and laughed – and hit the concrete wall at full speed, tumbling headfirst into the poo.

A half hour later a fleet of French police cars pulled into the farmyard. Their sirens blared. Their blue lights flashed. They screeched to a halt beside the helicopter, and the Power and Parfait families piled out. They expected the worst.

They found JP sitting on a bale of hay, eating an apple. Spread around him, munching bones and scratching themselves, were Hans and Butch and Mitzu and Axel and Lexa and Penelope and Pucker. And Espike, fast asleep. Beside the henhouse, wrapped up like chickens in a butcher shop window, were Ivan, Igor and Prunella.

'What's that smell?' Ted said.

'I think it's Prunella,' Clare said.

Prunella glared at them.

'Why is her hair so – awful?' Suzie said.

But Clare wasn't listening. 'Look at our hero!' she said, hugging JP. 'You did it, JP. You saved the day.'

'A true Power,' Ted said.

Paulette rushed from her parents and gave JP a big kiss. He turned as red as a ruby. But Suzie's eyes were crinkled. Something wasn't right.

'How exactly did you do it, JP?' she asked.

JP smiled. 'It was nothing.'

'Oh, really?'

She looked at Pucker, who was sitting beside Penelope, staring at her like a lovesick puppy.

Then he caught Suzie's eye. She could have sworn he winked at her.

But dogs don't wink, do they?

12

Party Time

The night before the Powers packed and departed from Paris, the Parfaits threw a party in their penthouse.

It was more than a party. It was a performance. A pageant. A pantomime.

Page-boys in purple pin-striped pyjamas served pepperoni pizza and pesto pasta and pickled pineapples. Paulette and JP played pass the parcel and pin the pink tail on the piggy. Pucker and Penelope peered into each other's eyes with puggly, poodley passion.

The Powers and Parfaits were perfectly pleasant to each other. The doggies danced and Don Mew mewed. Everyone was happy that the precious pets were back with their proud families, even Proteo, who turned himself into a pony and gave rides to children and small animals.

'What is that rumbling sound?' Ted said to Clare.

'Oh, that's Espike. One of Pucker's new friends. He's asleep under the table.'

'How can anyone sleep with all this noise?' Ted asked.

'Get used to it,' Clare said. 'Pucker has invited him to stay with us in Dublin on his way back to Guatemala. And from what I understand, he takes his time getting from A to B.'

'*Pucker* invited him?' Ted was taken aback.

'Well,' said Clare, 'the police told me he can't go back to Guatemala for a month, and I just know that Pucker would love to have him stay with us.'

'And what's the diddly-dory with that pair? They look like greyhounds gone wrong.'

Axel and Lexa were dancing, looking like a single hairless Afghan prancing in front of a mirror.

'Shh, Ted,' Clare said. 'Those evil men shaved them so that they wouldn't use their silky hair to make ropes to trip up – ah, never mind. It's too complicated.'

'Well, they look *cold*.'

'I know. And don't get annoyed, but Pucker also invited them to our house in Dublin. Afghanistan is freezing at this time of year.'

JP passed by on the pony. He couldn't see Don Mew, who was close behind, stalking him. 'Mad and Dumb, look at me!' JP said. 'I'm a bowcoy!'

'Mad and Dumb?'

'He means Dad and Mum.'

'Arrrrooooooooooo.'

'Janey mackers,' Ted said. 'What was *that*?'

'Pucker's friend Butch. He's from Texas and he's lonely and he's –'

'Don't tell me – Pucker has invited him to stay with us.'

'Ted – how did you guess?'

Mr Parfait lifted a wineglass and tapped it with a spoon until the room was quiet. He cleared his throat. '*Mesdames et Messieurs*, I would like to propose a toast.'

'Would that be a French toast?' Suzie asked.

'To Poo-care and Penelope. Welcome home. And to PJ –'

'JP,' Clare shouted.

'*Oui*, JP. For his birthday. *Joyeux anniversaire*.'

'*Joyeux anniversaire*,' everyone shouted, lifting their glasses.

'And please, everyone,' Mrs Parfait said, 'help yourself to birthday cake.'

The pony turned its head and said, 'Did someone say "cake"?'

Ping! The pony turned back into Proteo, who ran to the dessert table and helped himself to a double slice. JP, who had still been riding the pony, floated in the air for a moment before falling to the floor with a bang.

This was the moment Don Mew had been waiting for. He pounced on JP, digging his sharp claws into JP's trousers. JP screamed and shook his leg, but Don Mew wouldn't let go. Paulette shouted and pleaded, but it was no use. Before anyone could pull the cat away, JP took off in flight mode, bouncing and buzzing around the room before crashing through one of the big picture windows and zooming into the evening sky, with Don Mew hanging on for dear life.

Silence, except for Espike's snoring.

'Mon Dieu!' said Pierre.

'Don Mew!' said Paulette.

'What's new?' said Clare, wearily. 'Ted, do something.'

But Ted had had enough. He wasn't angry, but the stress, the noise, the dogs – it was all too much for him. Smoke streamed from the tips of his fingers and the toes of his shoes.

'Dad,' Suzie said, 'be careful.'

'I *am* careful. But this room is roasting.'

Cold air streamed through the broken window. 'Actually, Dad, it's freezing.'

A small fireball dropped from Ted's nose onto the Parfaits' lovely thick white carpet. Another one. A third. The carpet went up in flames like a trail of petrol.

Chaos. Fear.

'Mum,' Suzie shouted, 'the weather.'

Clare concentrated and in seconds heavy rain started lashing down from the ceiling, putting out the fire and soaking everyone except Espike, who still slept under the table. And just when Suzie breathed a sigh of relief, hailstones the size of plums fell, bonking everyone on the head before Suzie used her reverse weather to make them stop.

The Parfaits sat in the cold, sizzling room, soaked and stunned. The dogs were howling. Then, with another almighty crash, JP came flying back through the other window, shattering that as well before hitting the wall and sliding to the floor, Don Mew still clutching his leg with a look of terror on his face.

Ted brushed bits of ice and broken glass

from his jumper, turned to Mr and Mrs Parfait and said. 'It's been a pleasure. It really has. But we have a plane to catch.'

✦

The Powers drove to the airport in a minivan. JP sat up front with the driver, nursing his scratched leg. Ted, Clare and Suzie sat in the middle seat. And in the big back seat were ... eight dogs. All coming to Dublin (it was 'pets fly free day' on Ryanair).

'I suppose you're going to tell me that Pucker invited them all,' Ted said.

'Ah, now, Ted,' said Clare, 'don't be like that.'

He glanced back at Pucker and Penelope, who were rubbing noses. 'Look at the pair of them,' he said under his breath. 'Next thing you know we'll be having little Poogles all over the house.'

'Poogles?' JP said.

'Never mind, JP,' Clare said.

Suzie turned and leaned over the seat. She was so happy to have Pucker back. 'You sly little dog,' she said so that only Pucker could hear. 'What did you do to get Mum to invite all your new friends to Dublin?'

'She just did it,' Pucker said.

Suzie's eyes grew big as peaches. Was she hearing things? Was she going mad? Was Pucker *smiling*?

'Pucker,' she whispered, 'did you just *talk*?'

Pucker wiggled his nose.

'Pucker, say something else.'

He scratched his side.

'Pucker, *speak* to me.'

'Arf,' he said.

Fin

Kevin Stevens

Kevin Stevens has written grown-up books about bank robbers and jazz musicians but he also likes to write for kids. He helped create the Nightmare Club books for Little Island and wrote *The Powers* before deciding that Pucker needed his own book. And he can talk to dogs – though they have no idea what he is saying.

Sheena Dempsey

Sheena Dempsey is a children's author and illustrator from Cork. She often draws pictures of foxes and guinea pigs, rats and cats but her favourite animal to draw is the dog. For the illustrations in *Pucker Power* she used watercolour, paper and one black colouring pencil, which is now just a tiny stump. She lives in London with her partner Mick, and a wayward greyhound called Sandy.

So you want to read more about the Powers? Well, there's another book:

The Powers – The not-so-super Superheroes.

Another adventure with the Irish superhero family who have some incredible powers, but seem to be seriously lacking in any ability to control them. Dad sets his head on fire, Mum brings thunderstorms everywhere she goes, JP flies into the wall more often than the sky and Suzie has had enough of the lot of them! And what will happen when they go on holidays to West Cork and end up trying to save Ireland from some gold-hungry pirates?

978-1-908195-83-8 / £5.99

Oh, you've read *The Powers* already?

Well, there's a website too. It's powerful! It's got an animation with the Powers' own theme tune. And best of all (we think), it's got Suzie's blog on it. Read about her secret powers. Find out about her eyebrows. (No, that is not a mistake. We said eyebrows, we meant eyebrows.) And there's other stuff too. So what are you waiting for? **www.readthepowers.com**